Dr. Seuss

DOCTOR'S ORDERS

1 3 5 7 9 10 8 6 4 2

ISBN: 978-0-00-748950-3

This edition first published by HarperCollins Children's Books in 2012.

A CIP catalogue record for this title is available from the British Library.

Printed and bound in Hong Kong

Dr. Seuss
DOCTOR'S ORDERS

HarperCollins *Children's Books*

CONTENTS

THE CAT
IN
THE
HAT

The sun did not shine.

It was too wet to play.

So we sat in the house

All that cold, cold, wet day.

I sat there with Sally.

We sat there, we two.

And I said, "How I wish

We had something to do!"

Too wet to go out

And too cold to play ball.

So we sat in the house.

We did nothing at all.

So all we could do was to
Sit!
   Sit!
      Sit!
         Sit!
And we did not like it.
Not one little bit.

And then
Something went BUMP!
How that bump made us jump!

We looked!

Then we saw him step in on the mat!

We looked!

And we saw him!

The Cat in the Hat!

And he said to us,

"Why do you sit there like that?"

"I know it is wet

And the sun is not sunny.

But we can have

Lots of good fun that is funny!"

"I know some good games we could play,"

Said the cat.

"I know some new tricks,"

Said the Cat in the Hat.

"A lot of good tricks.

I will show them to you.

Your mother

Will not mind at all if I do."

Then Sally and I

Did not know what to say.

Our mother was out of the house

For the day.

But our fish said, "No! No!
Make that cat go away!
Tell that Cat in the Hat
You do NOT want to play.
He should not be here.
He should not be about.
He should not be here
When your mother is out!"

"Now! Now! Have no fear.
Have no fear!" said the cat.
"My tricks are not bad,"
Said the Cat in the Hat.
"Why, we can have
Lots of good fun, if you wish,
With a game that I call
Up-up-up with a fish!"

"Put me down!" said the fish.

"This is no fun at all!

Put me down!" said the fish.

"I do NOT wish to fall!"

"Have no fear!" said the cat.

"I will not let you fall.

I will hold you up high

As I stand on a ball.

With a book on one hand!

And a cup on my hat!

But that is not ALL I can do!"

Said the cat . . .

"Look at me!

Look at me now!" said the cat.

"With a cup and a cake

On the top of my hat!

I can hold up TWO books!

I can hold up the fish!

And a little toy ship!

And some milk on a dish!

And look!

I can hop up and down on the ball!

But that is not all!

Oh, no.

That is not all . . .

"Look at me!

Look at me!

Look at me NOW!

It is fun to have fun

But you have to know how.

I can hold up the cup

And the milk and the cake!

I can hold up these books!

And the fish on a rake!

I can hold the toy ship

And a little toy man!

And look! With my tail

I can hold a red fan!

I can fan with the fan

As I hop on the ball!

But that is not all.

Oh, no.

That is not all. . . ."

That is what the cat said . . .

Then he fell on his head!

He came down with a bump

From up there on the ball.

And Sally and I,

We saw ALL the things fall!

And our fish came down, too.

He fell into a pot!

He said, "Do I like this?

Oh, no! I do not.

This is not a good game,"

Said our fish as he lit.

"No, I do not like it,

Not one little bit!"

"Now look what you did!"

Said the fish to the cat.

"Now look at this house!

Look at this! Look at that!

You sank our toy ship,

Sank it deep in the cake.

You shook up our house

And you bent our new rake

You SHOULD NOT be here

When our mother is not.

You get out of this house!"

Said the fish in the pot.

"But I like to be here.

Oh, I like it a lot!"

Said the Cat in the Hat

To the fish in the pot.

"I will NOT go away.

I do NOT wish to go!

And so," said the Cat in the Hat,

"So

   so

     so . . .

I will show you

Another good game that I know!"

And then he ran out.

And, then, fast as a fox,

The Cat in the Hat

Came back in with a box.

A big red wood box.

It was shut with a hook.

"Now look at this trick,"

Said the cat.

"Take a look!"

Then he got up on top

With a tip of his hat.

"I call this game FUN-IN-A-BOX,"

Said the cat.

"In this box are two things

I will show to you now.

You will like these two things,"

Said the cat with a bow.

"I will pick up the hook.

You will see something new.

Two things. And I call them

Thing One and Thing Two.

These Things will not bite you.

They want to have fun."

Then, out of the box

Came Thing Two and Thing One!

And they ran to us fast.

They said, "How do you do?

Would you like to shake hands

With Thing One and Thing Two?"

And Sally and I

Did not know what to do.

So we had to shake hands

With Thing One and Thing Two.

We shook their two hands.

But our fish said, "No! No!

Those Things should not be

In this house! Make them go!

"They should not be here
When your mother is not!
Put them out! Put them out!"
Said the fish in the pot.

"Have no fear, little fish,"
Said the Cat in the Hat.
"These Things are good Things."
And he gave them a pat.
"They are tame. Oh, so tame!
They have come here to play.
They will give you some fun
On this wet, wet, wet day."

"Now, here is a game that they like,"
Said the cat.
"They like to fly kites,"
Said the Cat in the Hat.

"No! Not in the house!"

Said the fish in the pot.

"They should not fly kites

In a house! They should not.

Oh, the things they will bump!

Oh, the things they will hit!

Oh, I do not like it!

Not one little bit!"

Then Sally and I
Saw them run down the hall.
We saw those two Things
Bump their kites on the wall!
Bump! Thump! Thump! Bump!
Down the wall in the hall.

Thing Two and Thing One!

They ran up! They ran down!

On the string of one kite

We saw Mother's new gown!

Her gown with the dots

That are pink, white and red.

Then we saw one kite bump

On the head of her bed!

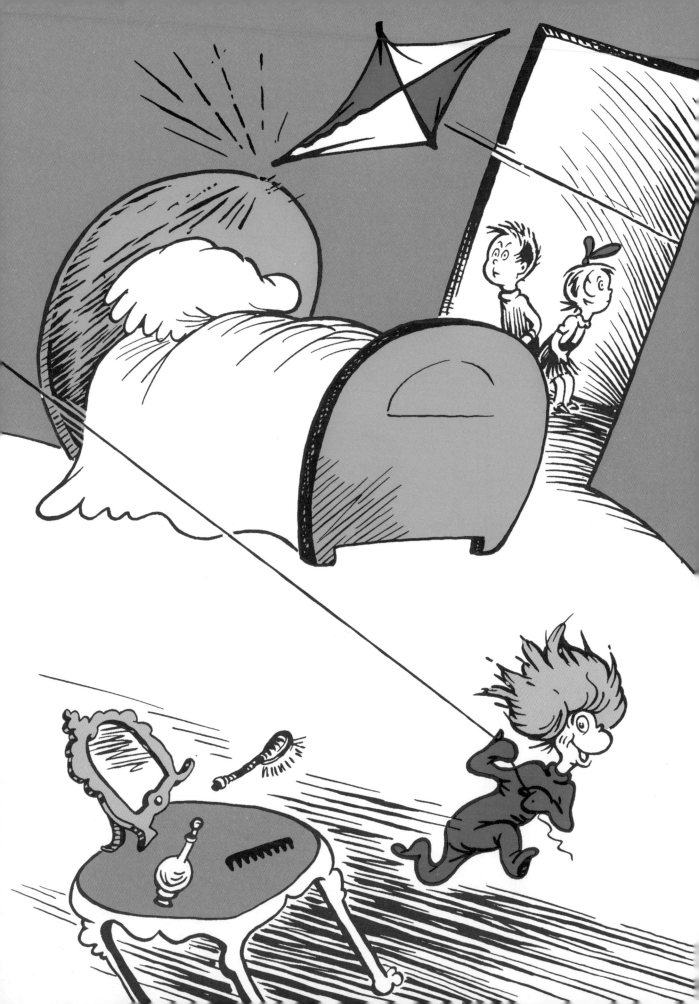

Then those Things ran about

With big bumps, jumps and kicks

And with hops and big thumps

And all kinds of bad tricks.

And I said,

"I do NOT like the way that they play!

If Mother could see this,

Oh, what would she say!"

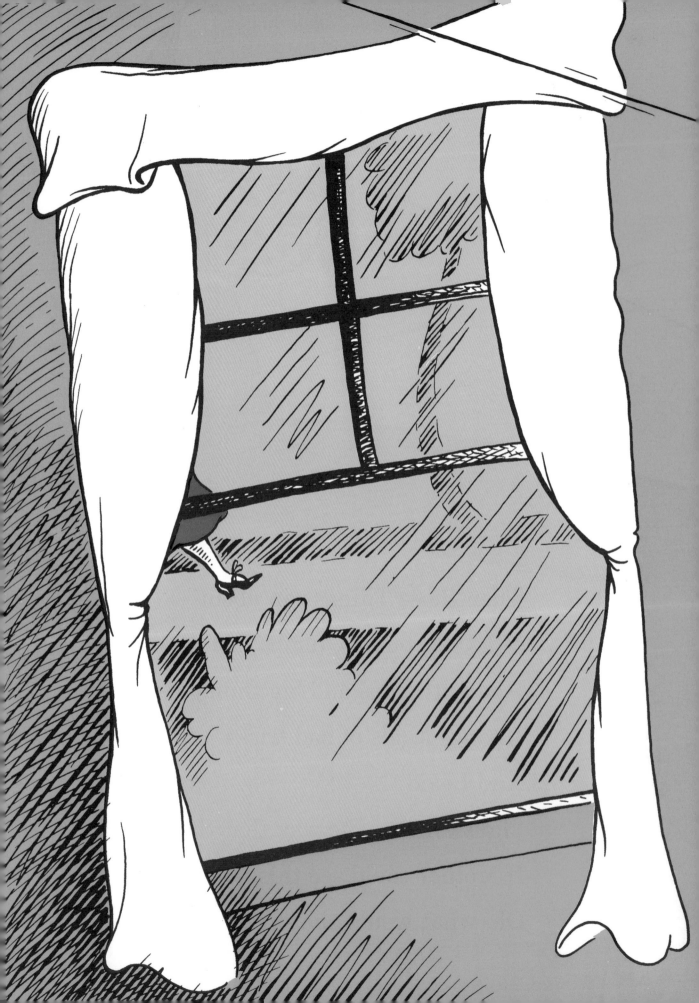

Then our fish said, "Look! Look!"

And our fish shook with fear.

"Your mother is on her way home!

Do you hear?

Oh, what will she do to us?

What will she say?

Oh, she will not like it

To find us this way!"

"So, DO something! Fast!" said the fish.

"Do you hear!

I saw her. Your mother!

Your mother is near!

So, as fast as you can,

Think of something to do!

You will have to get rid of

Thing One and Thing Two!"

So, as fast as I could,

I went after my net.

And I said, "With my net

I can get them I bet.

I bet, with my net,

I can get those Things yet!"

Then I let down my net.

It came down with a PLOP!

And I had them! At last!

Those two Things had to stop.

Then I said to the cat,

"Now you do as I say.

You pack up those Things

And you take them away!"

"Oh dear!" said the cat.

"You did not like our game . . .

Oh dear.

What a shame!

What a shame!

What a shame!"

Then he shut up the Things

In the box with the hook.

And the cat went away

With a sad kind of look.

"That is good," said the fish.

"He has gone away. Yes.

But your mother will come.

She will find this big mess!

And this mess is so big

And so deep and so tall,

We can not pick it up.

There is no way at all!"

And THEN!

Who was back in the house?

Why, the cat!

"Have no fear of this mess,"

Said the Cat in the Hat.

"I always pick up all my playthings

And so . . .

I will show you another

Good trick that I know!"

Then we saw him pick up

All the things that were down.

He picked up the cake,

And the rake, and the gown,

And the milk, and the strings,

And the books, and the dish,

And the fan, and the cup,

And the ship, and the fish.

And he put them away.

Then he said, "That is that."

And then he was gone

With a tip of his hat.

Then our mother came in
And she said to us two,
"Did you have any fun?
Tell me. What did you do?"

And Sally and I did not know
What to say.
Should we tell her
The things that went on there that day?

Should we tell her about it?

Now, what SHOULD we do?

Well . . .

What would YOU do

If your mother asked YOU?

Green Eggs and Ham

That Sam-I-am!

That Sam-I-am!

I do not like

that Sam-I-am!

Do you like

green eggs and ham?

I do not like them,
Sam-I-am.
I do not like
green eggs and ham.

Would you like them
here or there?

I would not like them
here or there.
I would not like them
anywhere.
I do not like
green eggs and ham.
I do not like them,
Sam-I-am.

Would you like them
in a house?
Would you like them
with a mouse?

I do not like them
in a house.
I do not like them
with a mouse.
I do not like them
here or there.
I do not like them
anywhere.
I do not like green eggs and ham.
I do not like them, Sam-I-am.

Would you eat them
in a box?
Would you eat them
with a fox?

Not in a box.

Not with a fox.

Not in a house.

Not with a mouse.

I would not eat them here or there.

I would not eat them anywhere.

I would not eat green eggs and ham.

I do not like them, Sam-I-am.

Would you? Could you?

In a car?

Eat them! Eat them!

Here they are.

I would not,
could not,
in a car.

You may like them.
You will see.
You may like them
in a tree!

I would not, could not in a tree.

Not in a car! You let me be.

I do not like them in a box.

I do not like them with a fox.

I do not like them in a house.

I do not like them with a mouse.

I do not like them here or there.

I do not like them anywhere.

I do not like green eggs and ham.

I do not like them, Sam-I-am.

A train! A train!
A train! A train!
Could you, would you,
on a train?

Not on a train! Not in a tree!
Not in a car! Sam! Let me be!

I would not, could not, in a box.
I could not, would not, with a fox.
I will not eat them with a mouse.
I will not eat them in a house.
I will not eat them here or there.
I will not eat them anywhere.
I do not eat green eggs and ham.
I do not like them, Sam-I-am.

Say!

In the dark?

Here in the dark!

Would you, could you, in the dark?

I would not, could not,
in the dark.

Would you, could you,
in the rain?

I would not, could not, in the rain.

Not in the dark. Not on a train.

Not in a car. Not in a tree.

I do not like them, Sam, you see.

Not in a house. Not in a box.

Not with a mouse. Not with a fox.

I will not eat them here or there.

I do not like them anywhere!

You do not like
green eggs and ham?

I do not
like them,
Sam-I-am.

Could you, would you,

with a goat?

I would not,
could not,
with a goat!

Would you, could you,

on a boat?

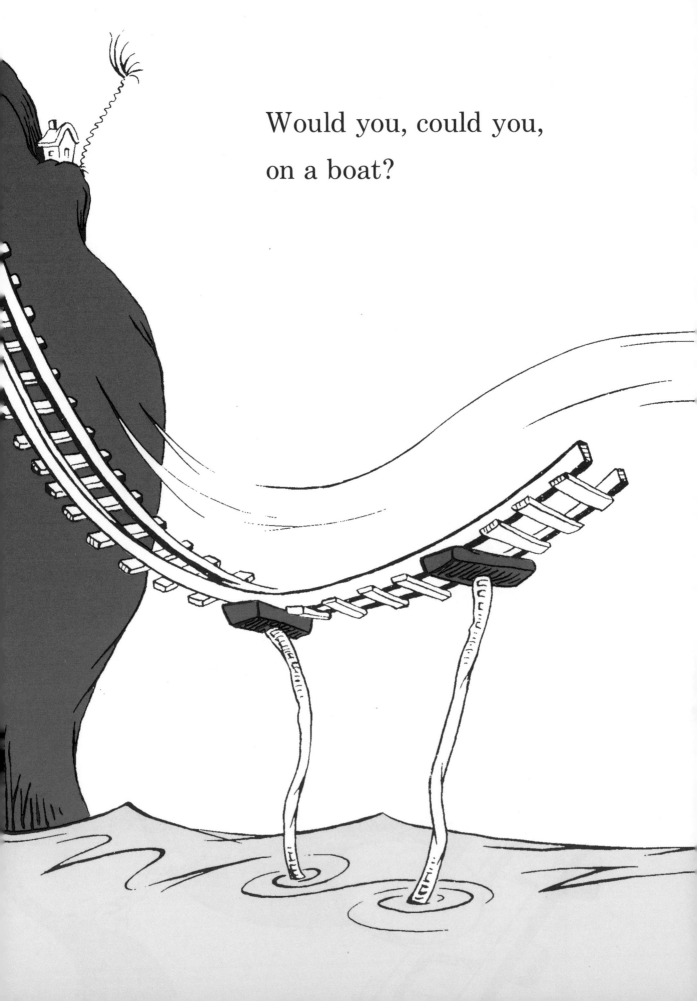

I could not, would not, on a boat.

I will not, will not, with a goat.

I will not eat them in the rain.

I will not eat them on a train.

Not in the dark! Not in a tree!

Not in a car! You let me be!

I do not like them in a box.

I do not like them with a fox.

I will not eat them in a house.

I do not like them with a mouse.

I do not like them here or there.

I do not like them ANYWHERE!

I do not like
green eggs
and ham!

I do not like them,
Sam-I-am.

You do not like them.

So you say.

Try them! Try them!

And you may.

Try them and you may, I say.

Sam!

If you will let me be,

I will try them.

You will see.

Sam!

I like green eggs and ham!

I do! I like them, Sam-I-am!

And I would eat them in a boat.

And I would eat them with a goat . . .

And I will eat them in the rain.

And in the dark. And on a train.

And in a car. And in a tree.

They are so good, so good, you see!

So I will eat them in a box.

And I will eat them with a fox.

And I will eat them in a house.

And I will eat them with a mouse.

And I will eat them here and there.

I will eat them ANYWHERE!

I do so like
green eggs and ham!
Thank you!
Thank you,
Sam-I-am!

Dr. Seuss's
ABC

BIG A

little a

What begins with A?

Aunt Annie's alligator . .

. . . . A . . a . . A

BIG B

little b

What begins with B?

Barber
baby
bubbles
and a
bumblebee.

BIG C

little c

What begins with C?

Camel on the ceiling
C . . . . c C

BIG D

little   d

David Donald Doo
dreamed
a dozen doughnuts
and
a duck-dog, too.

ABCDE..e..e

ear

egg

elephant

e

e

E

BIG **F**

little   f

F ... f ... F

Four fluffy feathers
on a
Fiffer-feffer-feff.

ABCD

EFG

Goat
girl
googoo goggles
G . . . g . . . G

BIG H

little   h

Hungry horse.
Hay.

Hen in a hat.
Hooray !
Hooray !

BIG I

little i

i . . . . i i

Icabod
is
itchy.

So am I.

BIG J

little   j

What begins with j?

Jerry Jordan's
jelly jar
and jam
begin that way.

BIG K

little k

Kitten. Kangaroo.

Kick a kettle.
Kite
and a
king's kerchoo.

BIG L

little   l

Little Lola Lopp.
Left leg.
Lazy lion
licks a lollipop.

BIG M

little   m

Many mumbling mice
are making
midnight music
in the moonlight . . .

mighty nice

BIG N
little n

What begins with those?

Nine new neckties
and a nightshirt
and a nose.

O is very useful.
You use it when you say:
"Oscar's only ostrich
oiled
an orange owl today."

ABCD
EFG
HIJK
LMNO...

...P

Painting pink pyjamas.
Policeman in a pail.

Peter Pepper's puppy.
And now
Papa's in the pail.

BIG Q
little q

What begins with Q ?

The quick
Queen of Quincy
and her
quacking quacker-oo.

QUACK

QUACK

BIG R

little   r

Rosy Robin Ross.

Rosy's going riding
on her
red rhinoceros.

BIG S

little s

Silly Sammy Slick
sipped six sodas
and got
sick sick sick.

T . . . . . T

t . . . . t

What begins with T ?

Ten tired turtles
on a tuttle-tuttle tree.

BIG U

little   u

What begins with U?

Uncle Ubb's umbrella
and his
underwear, too.

BIG V

little   v

Vera Violet Vinn
 is
very
very
very awful
on her violin.

W . . w . . W

Willy Waterloo
washes Warren Wiggins
who is
washing Waldo Woo.

X is very useful
if your name is
Nixie Knox.
It also
comes in handy
spelling axe
and extra fox.

NIXIE KNOX

BIG Y

little y

A yawning yellow yak.
Young Yolanda Yorgenson
is yelling on his back.

ABCD
EFG...

HIJK
LMNOP...

QRS
TUV...

W..X
Y.. and ....

BIG Z

little   z

What begins with Z?

I do.

I am a
Zizzer-Zazzer-Zuzz
as you can
plainly see.

*For
Lee Groo,
the Enunciator*

Said a book-reading parrot named Hooey,
"The words in this book are all phooey.
When you say them, your lips
will make slips and back flips
and your tongue may end up in Saint Looey!"

Do you like fresh fish?
It's just fine at Finney's Diner.
Finney also has some fresher fish
that's fresher and much finer.
But his best fish is his freshest fish
and Finney says with pride,
"The finest fish at Finney's
is my freshest fish, French-fried!"

SO . . .

don't order the fresh

or the fresher fish.

At Finney's, if you're wise,

you'll say,

"Fetch me the finest

French-fried freshest

fish that Finney fries!"

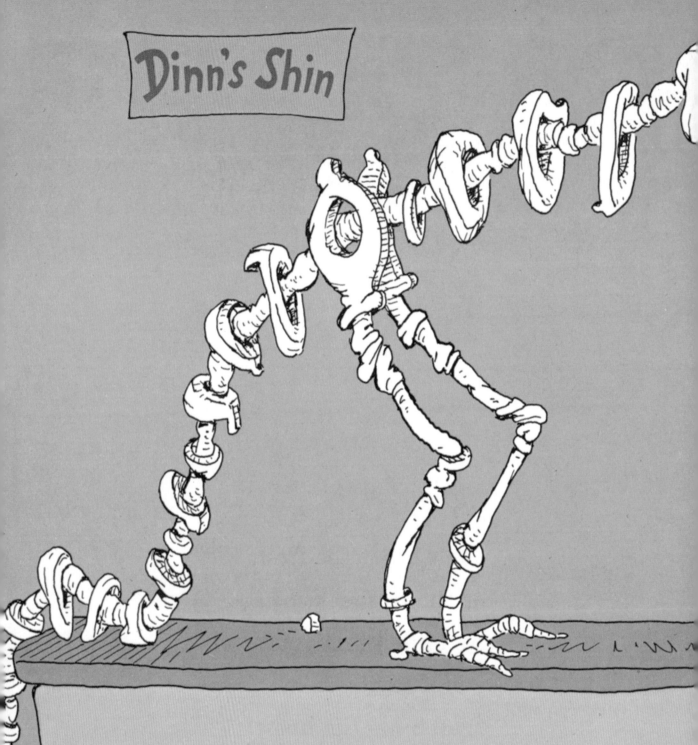

Dinn's Shin

We have a dinosaur named Dinn.

Dinn's thin. Dinn doesn't have much skin.

And the bones fall out

of his left front shin.

Then we have to call in Pinner Blinn,
who comes with his handy shin-pin bin
and with a thin Blinn shinbone pin,
Blinn pins Dinn's shinbones right back in.

Bed Spreaders spread spreads on beds.

Bread Spreaders spread butters on breads.

And that Bed Spreader better

watch out how he's spreading . . .

or that Bread Spreader's
sure going to butter his bedding.

Ape Cakes
Grape Cakes

As he gobbled the cakes on his plate,
the greedy ape said as he ate,
"The greener green grapes are,
the keener keen apes are
to gobble green grape cakes.
They're GREAT!"

Are you having trouble
in saying this stuff?
It's really quite easy for me.
I just look in my mirror
and see what I say,
and then I just say what I see.

Now let's talk about MONEY!

You should leave your Grox home
when you travel by air.
If you take him along,
they charge double the fare.
And your Grox must be packed
and locked up in a Grox Box,
which costs much, much more
than a little old fox box.
So it's heaps a lot cheaper
to fly with your foxes
than waste all that money
on boxes for Groxes.

And, what do you think costs more?...

A Simple Thimble

or

a Single Shingle?

A simple thimble <u>could</u> cost less
than a single shingle would, I guess.
So I think that the single shingle <u>should</u>
cost more than the simple thimble would.

If you like to eat potato chips
and chew pork chops on clipper ships,
I suggest that you chew
a few chips and a chop
at Skipper Zipp's Clipper Ship Chip Chop Shop.

And if your tongue
is getting queasy,
don't give up.
The next one's EASY!

There are so many things
that you really should know.
And that's why I'm bothering
telling you so.
You should know the first names
of the Fuddnuddler Brothers
who like to pile each on the heads of the others.
If you start at the top,
there are Bipper and Bud
and Skipper and Jipper
and Jeffrey and Jud,
Horatio, Horace and Hendrix and Hud,
and then come Dinwoodie and Dinty and Dud,
also Fitzsimmon and Frederick and Fud,
and Slinkey and Stinkey and Stuart and Stud.
And, down at the bottom
is poor little Lud.
But if Lud ever sneezes,
his name will be MUD.

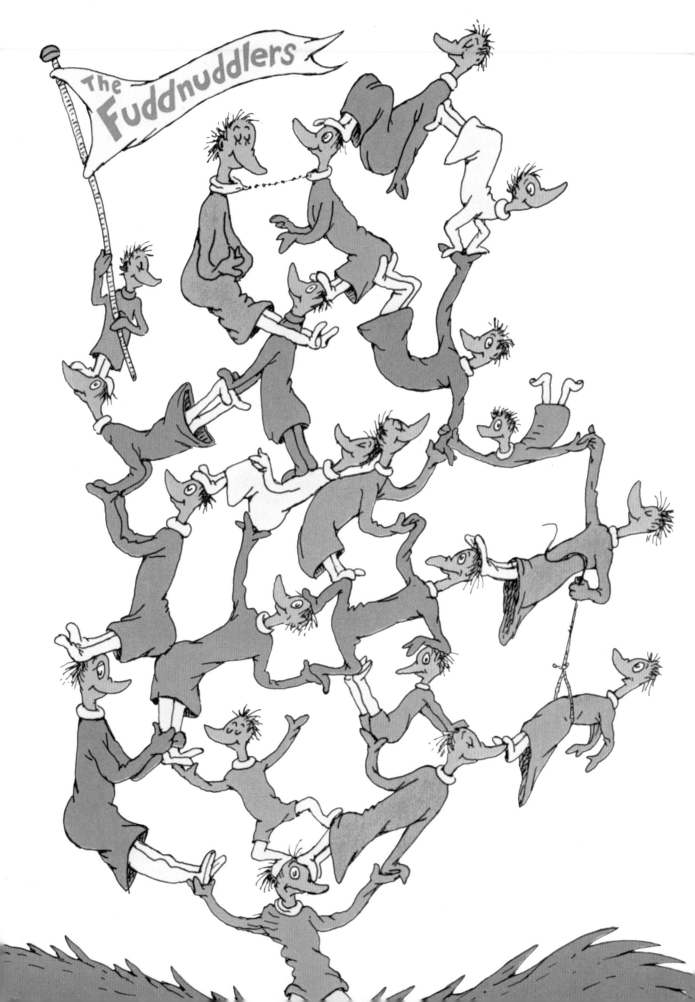

QUACK QUACK !

We have two ducks. One blue. One black.
And when our blue duck goes "Quack-quack"
our black duck quickly quack-quacks back.
The quacks Blue quacks make her quite a quacker
but Black is a quicker quacker-backer.

AND . . . speaking of quacks
reminds me of cracks
and stacks and sacks
and shacks and Schnacks.
SO . . . oh say can you say,
"I have cracks in my shack,
I have smoke in my stack,
and I think there's a Schnack
in the sack on my back!"

WEST BEAST

Upon an island hard to reach,

the East Beast sits upon his beach.

Upon the west beach sits the West Beast.

Each beach beast thinks he's the best beast.

EAST BEAST

Which beast is best? . . . Well, I thought at first
that the East was best and the West was worst.
Then I looked again from the west to the east
and I liked the beast on the east beach least.

Pete Pats Pigs

Pete Briggs pats pigs.

Briggs pats pink pigs.

Briggs pats big pigs.

(Don't ask me why. It doesn't matter.)

Pete Briggs is a pink pig, big pig patter.

Pete Briggs pats his big pink pigs all day.

(Don't ask me why. I cannot say.)

Then Pete puts his patted pigs away

in his Pete Briggs' Pink Pigs Big Pigs Pigpen.

Fritz needs Fred and Fred needs Fritz.

Fritz feeds Fred and Fred feeds Fritz.

Fred feeds Fritz with ritzy Fred food.

Fritz feeds Fred with ritzy Fritz food.

And Fritz, when fed, has often said,

"I'm a Fred-fed Fritz.

Fred's a Fritz-fed Fred."

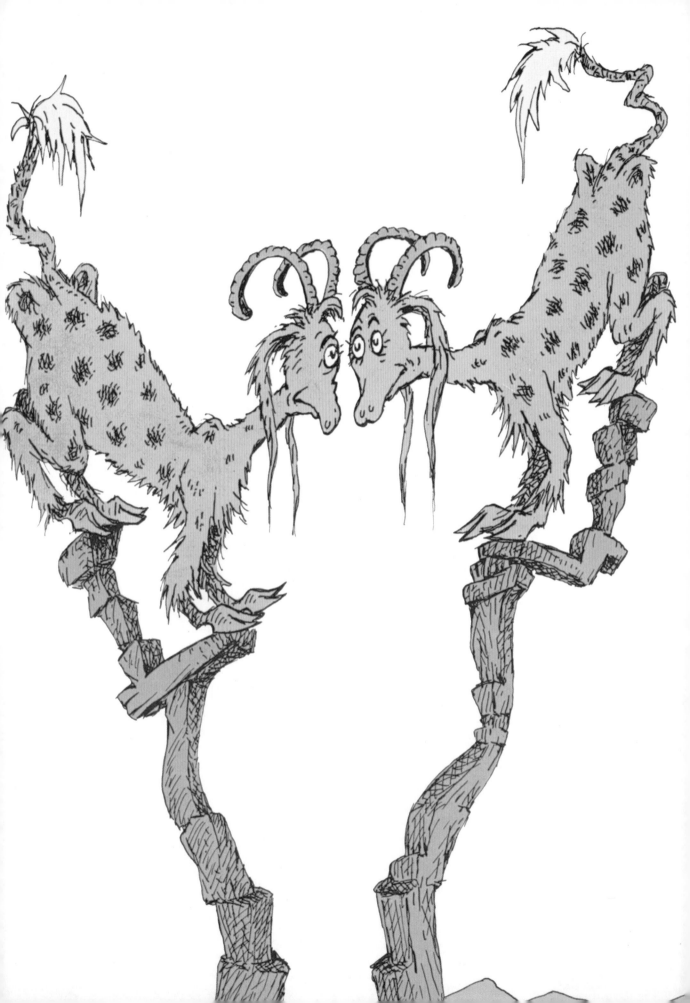

How to tell a Klotz from a Glotz

Well, the Glotz, you will notice,
has lots of black spots.
The Klotz is quite different
with lots of black dots.
But the big problem is
that the spots on a Glotz
are about the same size
as the dots on a Klotz.
So you first have to spot
who the one with the dots is.
Then it's easy to tell
who the Klotz or the Glotz is.

What would you rather be when you Grow Up?

A cop in a cop's cap?

Or a cupcake cook

in a cupcake cook's cap?

Or a fat flapjack flapper

in a flat flapped-jack cap?

OR . . .
if you think
you don't like cops' caps,
flapjack flappers'
or cupcake cooks' caps,
maybe you're one
of those choosy chaps
who likes kooky captains' caps
perhaps.

More about Blinn

Well, when Blinn comes home tired
from his work pinning shins,
the happiest hour of old Blinn's day begins.
Mr. Blinn is the father of musical twins
who, tucking twin instruments under twin chins,
lull their daddy to sleep with twin Blinn violins.

AND . . . oh say can you say,

"Far away in Berlin

a musical urchin named Gretchen von Schwinn

has a blue-footed, true-footed,

trick-fingered, slick-fingered,

six-fingered, six-stringed tin Schwinn mandolin."

Rope Soap
Hoop Soap

If you hope

to wash soup off a rope,

simply scrub it with SKROPE!

Skrope is so strong that no rope is too long!

But if you should wish to wash
soup off a hoop, I suggest that it's best
to let your whole silly souped-up hoop soak
in Soapy Cooper's Super Soup-Off-Hoops Soak Suds.

One year we had a Christmas brunch
with Merry Christmas Mush to munch.
But I don't think you'd care for such.
We didn't like to munch mush much.

And, speaking of Christmas...

Here are
some Great Gifts
to give to your daddy!

If your daddy's name is Jim
and if Jim swims and if Jim's slim,
the perfect Christmas gift for him
is a set of Slim Jim Swim Fins.

But if your daddy's name is Dwight
and he likes to look at birds at night,
the gift for Dwight that might be right
is a Bright Dwight Bird-Flight
Night-Sight Light.

A walrus with whiskers
is not a good pet.
And a walrus which whispers
is worse even yet.
When a walrus lisps whispers
through tough rough wet whiskers,
your poor daddy's ear
will get blispers and bliskers.

And that's almost enough
of such stuff for one day.
One more and you're finished.
Oh say can you say? . . .

"The storm starts
when the drops start dropping.
When the drops stop dropping
then the storm starts stopping."